THE
RHINELAND WAR:
1936

THE WAY IT MIGHT HAVE HAPPENED

Laszlo Solymar

authorHOUSE®

AuthorHouse™
1663 Liberty Drive
Bloomington, IN 47403
www.authorhouse.com
Phone: 1-800-839-8640

Published by AuthorHouse   10/18/2012

ISBN: 978-1-4772-3164-7 (sc)
ISBN: 978-1-4772-3165-4 (e)

THE
RHINELAND WAR:
1936

Laszlo Solymar was born and educated in Hungary. In the aftermath of the Hungarian Revolution he escaped to England. He joined the University of Oxford in 1966 where he is now an Emeritus Professor. During his career he had Visiting Professorships at the Universities of Paris, Copenhagen, Osnabruck, Berlin, Madrid and Budapest.

For all the grandchildren:
Tanya, Georgie, Oscar and Juliet.

Contents

ACT 1

THE AWAKENING

SCENE 1

NARRATOR: It was a bleak moment in history when the Great War started. 'The lamps are going out all over Europe; we shall not see them lit again in our lifetime', said the British Foreign Secretary. The lamps were lit again four years later but they were less bright and tended to go out when the wind blew from the wrong direction. Recovery from the carnage was slow and painful. The whole of Europe suffered, victor and vanquished alike. No more wars, said the people. Wars are fought with weapons. Get rid of the weapons and there will be no more wars. (PAUSE.) No more wars, said the diplomats of the victorious powers as they gathered in Paris to prepare the peace treaty. There will be no more wars if the martial tendencies of the Teutonic race can be curbed. Reduce the German Army to a bare minimum! Destroy the German arms industry! Ban German troops from the vicinity of the French border, and there will be no more wars. (PAUSE.) No more wars, declared leading members of the Labour Party. Abolish the evils of capitalism and

1

imperialism! Achieve world peace and socialism! War is morally incompatible with the conception of socialist faith, said George Lansbury, the Leader of the Labour Party. He was ready to confirm his views to a journalist.

JOURNALIST: Mr. Lansbury, how do you think peace could be preserved in the world today? What do you think Britain should do?

LANSBURY: I think we have been all wrong for centuries. The only path to peace is not to fight. Whether some people in this country like it or not we must give up all right to hold any other country, renounce all imperialism and stand unarmed before the world. We shall then become the strongest nation in the world, fully armed by justice and love.

NARRATOR: The revulsion against all kind of wars reached even the highest echelons of British society. It affected the flower of British youth at our most famous University.

USHER (LOUDLY PROCLAIMING): Resolution 1792 of the Oxford Union on the 9th February, 1933: 'This House will in no circumstances fight for its King and Country'. For 275, against 153. The resolution is carried.

SCENE 2

NARRATOR: Numerous were the men of peace; they made their protestations. But the men of war were unaffected by their pleas. It is not that war was their favourite pastime. No, it was more than that. War was their obsession. How to win the next war was all they cared about. One of these men was Captain Charles de Gaulle, a veteran of the Great War. He was a man of towering height, formidable energy, and boundless self-confidence. He also possessed a phenomenally large nose often compared with that of Cyrano de Bergerac.

NARRATOR 2 (FEMALE VOICE): Captain de Gaulle was sent to work for the Chief Secretariat for National Defence in France, a permanent body at the disposal of the Prime Minister, charged with preparing the state and the nation for war. He took his duties very seriously. His theory of warfare, not warfare in general but how the next war would be fought, was published in the spring of 1934. He was not in favour of the defensive strategy promoted at the time by the adherents of Marshall Petain. He advocated the establishment of a professional army and called attention to the crucial importance of mobility gained by the deployment of independent tank units.

JOURNALIST: Captain, do you think that God always helps the bigger armies?

DE GAULLE: No, not at all. He may consider helping a smaller army if it is well organised.

JOURNALIST: Who do you think we shall fight in the next war?

DE GAULLE: The Germans of course. Who else?

JOURNALIST: What do you think of Article 8 of the Covenant of the League of Nations?

DE GAULLE: What does it say?

JOURNALIST: The Members of the League recognise that the maintenance of peace requires the reduction of national armaments to the lowest level—

DE GAULLE: Nonsense.

JOURNALIST: Do I take it that you are against all forms of disarmament?

DE GAULLE: Am I allowed to quote someone else's words.

JOURNALIST: Whose?

DE GAULLE; Those of M. Painleve, twice our Prime Minister: 'France disarmed is not an example, it is a temptation.'

JOURNALIST: What do you think the priorities of our defence policy should be in the immediate future?

DE GAULLE: We must be prepared to take action outside our own country at any moment and in any eventuality. We must be ready to fight a preventive war too. We should be able to strike at the enemy while we still have the advantage.

JOURNALIST: Preventive war, has it got any moral justification? Do you believe in justice Captain?

DE GAULLE: Yes, I do. Occasionally though it might not be enough on its own. Justice without a sword by its scales soon falls into ridicule. Remember that, young man, when you next think of justice.

SCENE 3

NARRATOR: Meanwhile Germany, led by the firm hand of her Chancellor, Adolf Hitler, had made great advances in many fields. Unemployment, the curse of the Weimar Republic had been completely eliminated. Hitler's admirers came from far and wide. Among them was the grand old man of British politics, an indomitable adversary of

Germany during the Great War. He visited Hitler in the autumn of 1935 at his retreat in the Bavarian mountains.

JOURNALIST: Mr Lloyd George, is it true that you and the German Chancellor admire each other?

LLOYD GEORGE: I don't know about him but—

JOURNALIST: He wrote about you in his book, *Mein Kampf*, didn't he? He regarded you as a great orator.

LLOYD GEORGE: Yes, I am aware of that, but I did not visit him to seek flattery. I have had my fair share of flattery in this country.

JOURNALIST: How did he receive you?

LLOYD GEORGE: Most cordially. He came down the steps to welcome me.

JOURNALIST: How would you describe him?

LLOYD GEORGE: A great man. He is indeed a great man. I have now had a chance to see something of the tremendous change he has effected.

JOURNALIST: But how? At what price?

LLOYD GEORGE: Whatever one may think of his methods—and they are certainly not those of a Parliamentary democracy—there can be no doubt that he has achieved a marvellous transformation in the spirit of the people, in their attitude towards each other, and in their social and economic outlook. One man has accomplished this miracle. He is a born leader of men. A magnetic dynamic personality with a single-minded purpose, a resolute will, and a dauntless heart. He is the national Leader. He is also making them secure against that constant dread of starvation which is one of the most painful memories of the last years of the war and the first years of the Peace.

JOURNALIST: Do you think that Great Britain might be at war with Germany within the next five years?

LLOYD GEORGE: Quite impossible. The establishment of a German hegemony in Europe which was the aim and dream of the old pre-war militarism, is not even on the horizon of Nazism.

SCENE 4

NARRATOR: In the 1930s the peace of Europe rested on two pillars: the treaties of Versailles and Locarno. Articles 42 and 43 of the Versailles Treaty forbade Germany to maintain or construct fortifications or to keep any military personnel within a wide swathe of territory between the French border and a line of 50 km East of the Rhine. The Treaty of Locarno, signed seven years after the end of the Great War, was designed to maintain the peace by preserving the status quo. Article 4 of Locarno confirmed Articles 42 and 43 of Versailles.

NARRATOR 2 (FEMALE VOICE.): Under the energetic leadership of Adolf Hitler Germany was no longer willing to accept her inferior status. In March 1935, contrary to the treaties' stipulations, Germany introduced conscription. The signatories of the Locarno Treaty, France, Great Britain, Belgium and Italy issued a protest. The protest was ignored.

NARRATOR: By the end of 1935 Germany appeared strong enough for Hitler to consider his next move. He instructed the Army to prepare plans for the reoccupation of the Rhineland.

LIEUTENANT: You understand, Herr Oberst, that I am not criticising the plan. I am just asking for clarifications.

COLONEL: As your superior officer I have nothing to add to the orders you received; but considering our family ties, young man, I am willing to listen to you.

LIEUTENANT: I see no difficulties in moving my men to the bridge at Waderborn over the Prim but that's quite close to the French border.

COLONEL: Does it frighten you, Lieutenant?

LIEUTENANT: No, no, no but I ask you respectfully what shall we do if we meet units of the French Army?

COLONEL: You will receive instructions in good time.

LIEUTENANT: Attack? Resist? Retreat? I must know.

COLONEL: You will receive instructions in good time.

LIEUTENANT: Uncle, please, don't fob me off. What can I do with a company of inexperienced men and two anti-aircraft guns? It will be a disaster. It is madness. Why can't we wait for another year or two?

COLONEL: I thought it was your generation which was itching to fight.

LIEUTENANT: We are all ready to lay down our lives for the Fatherland but why such hurry? Our recruits are not ready yet.

COLONEL: A soldier does not question his orders.

LIEUTENANT: Uncle Thomas, please tell me, do you think this is the right time to move into the Rhineland? What if we fail?

COLONEL: That's enough, lieutenant. About-turn!

SCENE 5

NARRATOR: By the end of 1935 the government of Pierre Laval was in its last throes. He lost credibility as the principal author of the Hoare-Laval Pact, an attempt to resolve the Abyssinian conflict favouring the Italian dictator. Sir Samuel Hoare had already resigned. Laval managed to hold on until January, 1936. The next government was to be formed by Albert Sarraut. Before he took office he asked George Mandel to visit him.

SARRAUT: How good of you to come.

MANDEL: It is a pleasure to meet you.

SARRAUT: I presume you have heard the rumours that I might form the next administration.

MANDEL: Nothing specific.

SARRAUT: I have a proposal to make. Would you be prepared to continue as Minister of Posts, Telegraphs and Telephones?

MANDEL: It would be a great privilege to serve under you.

SARRAUT: Thank you, thank you. (PAUSE.) There's another thing I want to talk about.

MANDEL: Germany?

SARRAUT: Yes, Germany. You feel strongly about their rearmament programme, don't you?

MANDEL: Yes, I do.

SARRAUT: You have read the reports of our agents from Germany?

MANDEL: Yes, I have.

SARRAUT: You know then that the Germans might move troops into the Rhineland at any time in the next few months. If it happened what do you think we should do?

MANDEL: Hit them with all our might. That's what Clemenceau would have done. You know I was his Chief of Staff for a while. I suppose I inherited his abrasiveness and his obstinacy. Hit them hard.

SARRAUT: Would it be fair to the Germans? After all, they only seek equality with the other European powers.

MANDEL (RAISING HIS VOICE.): Fairness? Are rigged elections fair play? Is it fair that the Nazis lock up their political opponents in concentration camps? Is it fair that roaming gangs of the SA and SS murder people at will?

SARRAUT: No. I mean not at all.

MANDEL: Sorry for the outburst. I have become even more abrasive with age. I have developed some kind of irrational fear of the future. I strongly believe that we should immediately intervene because all that hullabaloo does not signify strength. It is just Hitler bluffing.

SARRAUT: You think so?

MANDEL: Yes, I do. Hitler is bluffing. There is actually a good German word for it: Vabanque-spiel. You can guess the meaning, can't you?

SARRAUT: With a bit of imagination, I can.

MANDEL: I am convinced that if we call his bluff we shall see the end of Germany's love affair with National Socialism. Hitler is a madman. Any clear-thinking strategist would advise him: 'Wait, until we are strong enough'. The fact that he is not willing to wait is a clear indication that he overruled the military analysts. He wants to keep up the momentum. He wants instant glory, and for that he is willing to take a gamble, a Vabanque-spiel. He is gambling on our inability to act quickly, gambling on our likely desire to refer the whole thing to the League of Nations, gambling on the conflicts in our own midst, gambling on our old-fashioned military strategy, gambling on the reluctance of the British to get involved, gambling on—

SARRAUT: So you want a military response?

MANDEL: If we respond immediately, without delay, and respond with overwhelming force they will not call up their reserves; they will flee like frightened rabbits. The Army will take over in no time. The great adventurer will be arrested. Don't forget that the Army is still led by the same generals, by the same officers, as during the Weimar Republic. Most of them had their training during Imperial times. They hate this clown; they will follow him as long as he is successful but will turn against him if he leads the army into a quagmire, into a shameful retreat. The German military don't like to lose prestige.

SARRAUT: Nor do we.

MANDEL: Nor do we but that is irrelevant now. A humiliated Army will never forgive Hitler. Nor will politicians of the old school who now toe the Nazi line with such enthusiasm. They are fair-weather friends. They will desert him in no time at all. With Hitler under house arrest we'll have nothing more to do in the Rhineland. We shall be able to afford the grand gesture of withdrawing our troops.

SCENE 6

NARRATOR: Sarraut formed his Cabinet on the 24th January 1936. One of the first things he did was to consult General Maurin, his Minister of War.

SARRAUT: You know the threat we are under. What do you think we could do?

MAURIN: I am well aware of the threat but regrettably our options are very limited.

SARRAUT: Can we take the offensive?

MAURIN: If the Germans move men and material into the Rhineland it would be practically impossible to dislodge them.

SARRAUT: Do I understand that you are unwilling to take the offensive?

MAURIN: Unwilling? No. I would love to take the offensive. Alas, we are not strong enough. And it is true of course that taking the offensive would be entirely contrary to logic and to our recent history. How can we think of taking the offensive when we have spent milliards to establish a fortified barrier? Are we so mad as to advance in front of this barrier? That would be a dangerous adventure, an adventure of the worst kind.

SARRAUT: I also meant to ask you about tanks. Paul Reynaud, I talked to him, he believes we sorely need them.

MAURIN: Yes, I know, Reynaud spoke in the Chamber about the need for mobile forces. He was put up to it by that arrogant young Staff Officer at the Chief Secretariat whose name I cannot recall at the moment.

SARRAUT: What is our present strength?

MAURIN: Many old ones, may be sixty or seventy B1, our high quality Char de bataille, and there is the new Somua-35. In spite of the cuts in the defence budget we have managed to enter four of them into service last month.

SARRAUT: Any chance that production can be stepped up?

MAURIN: No chance. No chance at all.

SARRAUT: Can we count on support from the British? Their tanks did pretty well at Cambrai in November '17 and their very successful 8th August offensive was led by hundreds of first class tanks.

MAURIN: That was in 1918. Since then they have been pondering a lot about armoured vehicles and have been writing long treatises about them. True they have put some of their new tanks on display but they have hardly anything ready for combat, may be one brigade. As a high ranking British officer recently told me, 'weight by weight we have more tank literature than tanks.' No, we can't count on them.

SARRAUT: So what is the best we can do?

MAURIN: Fortify our defences. That's the proper military response to the German Army appearing on our door-step.

SARRAUT: And what if the next war starts by the Germans attacking again through Belgium? That border is entirely unprotected.

MAURIN: Next time the Germans will not attack through Belgium. I am sure of that. A range of mountains such as the Ardennes are as good a barrier as the Maginot Line. And that's not only my opinion. That's part of the strategy developed by Marshall Petain himself.

SARRAUT: So there's no way of standing up to the
Germans?

MAURIN: Well, we could consider general mobilisation
but that is too drastic a step. And what would we
achieve with it? Frighten the Germans? War would
then become inevitable. But apart from everything
else, do you really want a general mobilisation so
close to the elections?

SARRAUT: We'll see, we'll see. Now to the relative strengths.
How do you estimate the strength of the German
armed forces relative to ours?

MAURIN: I think they have reached parity in manpower
and superiority in a number of other fields,
particularly in the air.

SARRAUT: And what's your estimate of the relative
strengths in a year's time?

MAURIN: We shall be outnumbered in every field.

SARRAUT: Isn't that an argument in favour of acting now?
This may be our last chance.

MAURIN: I realise the gravity of having German troops
on the left bank of the Rhine but I don't think
we should act. I don't think we can act. We may
precipitate a war none of us wants. We have built
an impenetrable line of fortifications. We have built
it with the explicit purpose of creating a barrier
against a German assault. Let's put our trust in it.

SARRAUT: A last question. As retribution for the
reoccupation, if it comes to that, could we
demonstrate a show of strength, anywhere?

MAURIN: I don't see any possibilities.

SARRAUT: Surely, we could overrun the German naval
base at Helgoland. It is in an exposed position far

away from the German mainland and the German Navy is far inferior to ours. Isn't that true?

MAURIN: Yes, that is true and it might be technically possible to occupy Helgoland but that would precipitate war for which we are not ready. France cannot afford to conduct an adventurous policy. We have to act within our means.

SCENE 7

SARRAUT (ON HIS OWN): Bloody defeatist! Contemptible coward! Has there ever been in the history of France a military leadership so afraid of war, so reluctant to fight? The destiny of France cannot be left in the hands of these generals. Clemenceau, the Tiger, was right. 'War is much too serious a thing to be left to the soldiers'. Some people say it's a clever aphorism, a bon mot. No, it is just the recognition of necessity. We cannot work with our present lot of generals. We need new blood, we need it soon, we need it now.

SCENE 8

NARRATOR: The anxiety about possible German action reached the other side of the Channel as well. The Prime Minister, Stanley Baldwin, and the Chancellor of the Exchequer, Neville Chamberlain, discussed the matter at Chequers.

BALDWIN: If the Germans invade the Rhineland what do you think we can do?

CHAMBERLAIN: You know as well as I do that our options are rather limited. We may not be able to do more than register a strong protest.

BALDWIN: We protested last year when Hitler introduced general conscription-to no avail.

CHAMBERLAIN: This time we shall make an even stronger protest. What else?

BALDWIN: Maybe, that's all we can do. I am worried, though, about the French. They might do something really stupid.

CHAMBERLAIN: I doubt it. They have been consulting us in the past and they will consult us in the future. At worst they will make some loud noises and then slowly, imperceptibly they will get over it.

BALDWIN: I actually have some sympathy with the Germans. No, I don't mean sympathy, I mean I can understand them. They are unwilling to keep on paying the price for losing the Great War-and who can blame them? How can we prevent them from moving troops into the Rhineland? Wouldn't we be furious if someone told us never to sail a warship into Plymouth harbour?

CHAMBERLAIN: Let's be fair. The clauses of the Versailles Treaty were far too harsh, unnecessarily harsh. We pointed it out at the time. The Americans never ratified the Treaty, did they? I don't think the concept of fairness ever entered the French mind. 'Exact revenge', that's all they could think of. 'Kick the Germans in the groin'—that has been their sole policy since the end of the war without any regard to German suffering. Poincare's decision to move troops into the Rhineland in 1923 was motivated by the same desire to mete out further punishment to the Germans. Now they are going to reap the bitter fruits of their policies. It is a miracle that the Germans have acted with such restraint in the last three years.

BALDWIN: Still, we must stand by the French.

CHAMBERLAIN: Yes, we must. If Hitler moves troops into the Rhineland we shall appeal to the League of Nations for redress. That appeal should ideally be lodged by all the Locarno powers jointly, by France, Italy, Belgium and ourselves.

BALDWIN: We may not be able to count on Italy after we were instrumental in imposing sanctions on them. Damn that Abyssinian affair! Not that it would make any difference. Whether Italy comes on board or not, we must raise the matter at the League of Nations.

CHAMBERLAIN: Yes, (PAUSE.) Yes. We shall of course fail. Whatever decision is reached the Germans will not accept it. I suppose we could ask the League to impose sanctions.

BALDWIN: No sanctions. There's no point in imposing sanctions.

CHAMBERLAIN: I agree. No sanctions. We do not want to alienate the Germans. If we fail at the League of Nations that should not preclude further negotiations with Hitler. I think I could do business with him. He is not such a danger to civilisation as people like Winston make out. I would not of course regard him as a great man. Certainly not the way Lloyd George has described him. The old man is losing his marbles, don't you think?

BALDWIN: He is not much older than we are.

CHAMBERLAIN: Yes, yes, but we are in full possessions of our marbles, aren't we?

BALDWIN: Well, I do feel occasionally some shortage of marbles but on the whole, yes, we are making sensible decisions. What do I think of Hitler? He is a nuisance. I would not be surprised if in the long run he caused us as much headache as Mussolini does now. We'll manage though. Our job is to preserve the British Empire intact. We need patience to wait until the storm blows over.

CHAMBERLAIN: Patience, yes, but the British Empire might not stay entirely intact. I would be quite happy to give Herr Hitler back a couple of colonies if that ensured peace in our time.

BALDWIN: Perhaps, perhaps. We may not need to go that far. We just have to play our cards right.

CHAMBERLAIN: What if the French demand action?

BALDWIN: You mean immediate military action?

CHAMBERLAIN: Yes.

BALDWIN: We'll tell them to calm down.

CHAMBERLAIN: What if they call upon us to discharge our treaty obligations without any reference to the League of Nations?

BALDWIN: I hope they won't.

CHAMBERLAIN: But what if they do?

BALDWIN: We could tell them that some of those Articles are a little ambiguous. You know which one I am referring to.

CHAMBERLAIN: Article 4 of Locarno?

BALDWIN: Yes, Article 4. I have the text. It says, 'In case of a flagrant violation of the present Treaty or of a flagrant breach of Articles 42 and 43 of the Treaty of Versailles by one of the High Contracting

Parties, each of the other Contracting Parties hereby undertakes immediately to come to the help of the Party against whom such a violation or breach has been directed'. Will this let us off the hook? What is a flagrant violation? Moving into their own backyard-is that a flagrant violation?

CHAMBERLAIN: It probably is.

BALDWIN: You don't think there is any possibility of wriggling out of it?

CHAMBERLAIN: I don't see any. We signed a solemn treaty, didn't we? In fact you may recall that you were Prime Minister at the time—

BALDWIN: You know that I have never taken any interest in foreign affairs. (SMILING.) It was all done by your brother, Austen.

CHAMBERLAIN: Half-brother.

BALDWIN: Whether a half-brother or full brother, he signed the treaty, and if I remember correctly we made him afterwards a Knight of the Garter in recognition of his services as its chief *accoucheur*.

CHAMBERLAIN: Well, then, we cannot possibly repudiate his signature, can we?

BALDWIN: No, we can't. It worries me though. You know what Lord Birkenhead said of your brother.

CHAMBERLAIN: Austen always played the game and always lost it. I hope it does not apply to Locarno.

BALDWIN: I hope so too. We'll see what happens. But I can tell you one thing: I shall never lead this country into war. It must be somebody else.

CHAMBERLAIN: We shall cross our bridges when we come to them. Meanwhile we just need to dissuade the French from doing anything stupid. We may need a little diplomacy.

BALDWIN: We may need a lot of diplomacy. That's what Foreign Secretaries are supposed to do. Eden is in constant contact with Flandin, isn't he?

CHAMBERLAIN: Yes, he is. I don't think we shall have any trouble. Clearly, we should take the case to the League of Nations. That's what the League is for. In fact, we can't do anything else but to put our trust in the League of Nations. I hope Eden has told Flandin not to upset the apple-cart.

BALDWIN: I am sure he did, though perhaps not in the same words. What is the French for apple-cart anyway?

SCENE 9

NARRATOR: The great majority of people in the British Isles were horrified by the prospect of war. They were strongly behind the policy of Baldwin and Chamberlain. But there were a few exceptions. Winston Churchill and the small group around him had been clamouring for years for a tougher line against the Germans, and demanding speedy rearmament.

JOURNALIST: What is the reason, Mr. Churchill, that you are so strongly opposed to the aspirations of Germany to take her rightful place at the table of European nations.

CHURCHILL: I may be slightly better at recognising danger signals than others. I visited Germany in '32. I was impressed-not favourably I have to add. I saw bands of Teutonic youths, marching through the streets and roads with the light of desire in their eyes to suffer for the Fatherland.

JOURNALIST: So you think they should continue suffering for the sins of their fathers.

CHURCHILL: That's not what I said. I am simply worried when I see people, particularly young people, ready to sacrifice themselves.

JOURNALIST: But surely you must agree that the restrictions still imposed upon Germany are unjust. Justice does not become injustice because it is demanded by a dictator or does it?

CHURCHILL: I don't wish to formulate the problem in terms of justice and injustice. My concern is to protect Britain, the British Empire and the whole civilised world.

JOURNALIST: There have been rumours circulating, particularly in France, that Germany wishes to renounce the Treaty of Locarno—

CHURCHILL: A treaty freely negotiated—

JOURNALIST: And move troops into the demilitarised zone. What kind of action do you think the Government should take?

CHURCHILL: It is not a question that anyone can answer in the abstract. We shall have to see what happens.

JOURNALIST: If the Rhineland is reoccupied what do you think the consequences will be for European politics?

CHURCHILL: Disastrous. You don't need to be a great strategist to see them. As soon as Herr Hitler's forces take possession of the left bank of the Rhine they will immediately set about building fortifications and that will, I regret, produce reactions across Europe. It will be a barrier across Germany's front door which will leave her free to sally out eastwards and southwards by the other doors. That is a less direct danger to us, but it is a more imminent danger.

The moment those fortifications are completed the whole aspect of Central Europe is changed. I am talking about the Baltic States, Poland, Czechoslovakia, Yugoslavia, Rumania and Austria. They will realize that France cannot enter German territory, they will realise that they are vulnerable, and consequently, all these countries will begin to feel very differently about their foreign policies. They will slowly discover virtues in Herr Hitler that had not been before so vividly perceived.

JOURNALIST: Do you think we can count on the Little Entente now?

CHURCHILL: Czechoslovakia, Rumania, Yugoslavia. Yes, we can count on them at the moment. We shall not be able to count on their support in the future if we allow German troops to enter and then to remain in the Rhineland. For the West the danger is equally great but perhaps not as imminent. The creation of a line of forts opposite the French frontier will allow the German troops to be reduced on that line, and will enable their main forces to swing round through Belgium and Holland. These are prospects I don't relish.

END OF ACT ONE

ACT 2

THE DECISION

SCENE 1

NARRATOR: On the morning of Saturday, 7th March, German military units moved into the demilitarised zone. Within the hour, Albert Sarraut, President of the Council of Ministers, called three members of his Cabinet, three members he could count on, to his office at the Hotel Matignon. They were Etienne Flandin, Joseph Paul-Boncour and Georges Mandel.

SARRAUT: Gentlemen, you've heard the news. We are in the ridiculous situation that a long-expected event suddenly occurs and we have no agreed policy to deal with it. I hope it is not too late. If the four of us could come up with a plan, I think we have a good chance of taking the Cabinet with us. To begin with, there is a decent argument in favour of doing nothing but to issue a strongly worded protest. That would make our generals deliriously happy. I don't believe, however, that it is our duty to care for the well-being of our generals. Can we reject this first option?

ALL (MURMURS OF APPROVAL): Yes . . . of course . . . we must . . .

SARRAUT: Our second option is to refer the whole thing to the League of Nations. We could propose putting all our armed forces, the Army, the Navy and the Air Force at the disposal of the League.

FLANDIN: You think the League of Nations would be capable of prompt action?

SARRAUT: We can call an emergency session. I believe they would act relatively quickly. The German action will be condemned in a week, nine days, perhaps eleven days, who knows? Have we got the time? The longer we leave it, the more difficult it will be to dislodge them.

MANDEL: My fear is that if we take the case to the League of Nations we shall have to be reasonable: lean backwards to save the peace of Europe, give every opportunity to the aggressors to explain their actions. We might have a decision in a week, if we are extremely lucky, but that will not force the Germans to withdraw. That will be only the first step in a long process. We can't wait. We must act immediately. Send them an ultimatum today and give them two days to clear out.

SARRAUT: Ultimatum today? No, that does not seem feasible. But I agree with the spirit of your proposal. We must resist the Germans. Do we all agree?

PAUL-BONCOUR: I would not give up so easily on the League of Nations. If we ask for an emergency session today, the Council will consider our complaint on, say, Tuesday. A decision might be reached by Friday or Saturday. That does not seem unreasonable to me. We should be able to wait until then. It is bound to lead to the condemnation of the German action. If the Council finds that the case we have put forward is just but is unable to offer us any satisfaction, the Covenant of the League of Nations will have been proved a fraud. If no means of lawful redress can be offered to an aggrieved party, the whole doctrine of international law and cooperation upon which the hopes of the future are based would lapse ignominiously. On the other hand, if the League of Nations were able to enforce its decree upon one of the most powerful countries in the world and declared it to be an aggressor, then the authority of the League would henceforth be accepted as the sovereign authority by which all international quarrels should be determined and controlled.

MANDEL: The Council will never go as far as to authorise military action without weeks and weeks of delay, dithering, vacillation. We have to act on our own.

FLANDIN: Is there any reason why we could not proceed with our two options simultaneously? We appeal to the League today but meanwhile prepare the military option. We could ask for an emergency session of the Council. London might be a convenient venue.

SARRAUT: Yes, we could do that. We are not losing any momentum by putting into motion the mechanisms at the League of Nations. As for fighting, I am all in favour in spite of the lukewarm support of our military. I think we need to test the mood of the country. My intention is to address the nation by radio tonight. It will be short and uncompromising. By the way, we need a few memorable phrases which people will repeat. What about this one: 'We are not disposed to allow our cities to come under the fire of German guns once more'? What do you think?

PAUL-BONCOUR: Good but perhaps we could make it more specific by referring to a particular city.

FLANDIN: Strasbourg?

SARRAUT: We are not disposed to allow Strasbourg to come under the fire of German guns. That's good. And I shall appeal to our patriotism. The Germans have obviously counted on the internal divisions we have had for years. I shall have to disabuse them. What about this: The national confusion stemming from our internal divisions explains the German Government's sudden decision. They forget yet again that at every grave hour of our history such confusion gives way to the immediate union of French energies, of the will of all parties to defend national independence and security. And so on, carry on in the same vein. Then finish with the sentence. 'The French people remain ready, in any circumstances, to demonstrate that their differences do not lead to their abdication and subjection'. What do you think?

ALL (MURMURS OF APROVAL): Good . . . good fighting stuff . . . I like it . . .

FLANDIN: Couldn't we make it a bit stronger?

SARRAUT: I think it is strong enough.

FLANDIN: Perhaps we should refer to the fait accompli—

SARRAUT: Yes, good idea. That's what we have: a brutal fait accompli. (TO FLANDIN DIRECTLY): Do you think the Foreign Office could prepare a speech for me by this afternoon based on such sentiments? You can have my notes.

FLANDIN: Yes, certainly.

SARRAUT: Now how can we win over the Cabinet? I shall have to declare national emergency and call an emergency session of the Chamber with the specific aim of strengthening the Cabinet with a few well-known individuals.

FLANDIN: Who do you have in mind?

SARRAUT: Paul Reynaud and Louis Barthou.

PAUL-BONCOUR: Barthou is confined to a wheel chair. He has not spoken in the Senate since he managed to survive that attempt on his life eighteen months ago.

SARRAUT: I know him. I talked to him not long ago. He will join us and he will use his influence.

MANDEL: He would indeed be a great asset. If we allow the Germans to remilitarise the Rhineland all Barthou's efforts at securing assistance from Central and Eastern Europe would go up in smoke. He will be with us.

FLANDIN: And Reynaud? It is many years since he last served in a Cabinet.

SARRAUT: Reynaud we can count on. He has made several speeches in the Chamber in favour of rapid rearmament and particularly in favour of a rapid response force, independent tank units, that kind of thing.

FLANDIN: I believe that whole idea came from a young officer at the Chief Secretariat for National Defence.

MANDEL: Not much has come out of that establishment.

FLANDIN: That young officer has got his heart in the right place. I've read a few extracts here and there from his book. In spite of a lot of emotional nonsense he makes a good case for mobility and, what concerns us most at the moment, for being prepared to fight an offensive war. Just one more point. I think we should avoid a total break with those who might like to come to some agreement with the dictators. What about co-opting Laval as well?

SARRAUT: Laval?

FLANDIN: Why not? After the failure of the Hoare-Laval proposals he is in a rather weak position. He will oppose intervention but he will not be able to sway the Cabinet.

SARRAUT: What do you think M. Mandel?

MANDEL: I am no great friend of Pierre Laval but M. Flandin has a point. The war Cabinet will look more credible with Laval in it. I presume Laval in is better than Laval out.

SARRAUT: So have we agreed? Barthou, Reynaud and Laval? (PAUSE.) I shall call them.

SCENE 2

NARRATOR: Nervously, Hitler waited for the first reactions to the occupation of the Rhineland. The special train in which he travelled to Munich was charged, compartment after compartment, with the tense atmosphere that emanated from the Fuhrer's section. Relief was provided by Dr. Goebbels, Minister of Propaganda and National Enlightenment in the Third Reich.

GOEBBELS (SPEAKING ON THE TELEPHONE): Mein Fuhrer, good news. France has appealed to the Council of the League of Nations. Your genius, your intuition, mein Fuhrer, has proved right once again. We have nothing to worry about. There will be long speeches accusing us of the violation of Article this and Article that, and then those armchair warriors, those shambolic democrats, those bumbling idiots will want to appear fair and will invite us to present our case. We'll send them our faithful Ribbentrop who will refute the charges one by one, and then the Council will have its field day with everybody carefully assessing all that can be assessed, and then they will bring forward a resolution condemning us as treaty-breakers, and then we shall wait a few days before sending any response, to give them a chance to shit in their pants, and after that we shall make our counter-proposals which they will send to a number of committees and sub-committees, and by the time the committees report everyone will have lost interest. Give it another month and we shall have the French and the British queuing up to propose treaties to us. Yes . . . , yes . . . , yes, mein Fuhrer. Heil Hitler.

SCENE 3

CHAMBERLAIN: The French are on the warpath again. What do you make of Sarraut's speech?

BALDWIN: I have read the transcript. What do I think of it? Typical Gallic rhetoric. Mind you, I quite like that sentence 'Nous ne sommes pas disposes a voir placer Strasbourg sous le feu des canons allemands'. Pure rhetoric. Why Strasbourg in particular?

CHAMBERLAIN: I like the one on fait accompli. 'We have been confronted with a fait accompli in its most brutal form.' That's what he says. He is right, of course but so pompous. And the warning to the Germans: 'They forget yet again that at every grave hour of our history'—D'you see it? 'Yet again'. A clear reference to 1914. French rhetoric at its best.

BALDWIN: Or at its worst? At its most meaningless?

CHAMBERLAIN (SARCASTICALLY): So passionate. Sounds like an oration from Winston. And with the same irresponsibility. The trouble with the French is that they speak first and think afterwards.

BALDWIN: Let them be pompous. I shall be worried when they act first and think afterwards. D'you think that they might do something stupid?

CHAMBERLAIN: The worst thing they could do is to order a general mobilisation.

BALDWIN: They won't do that. Not before an election. They can't do that. They know very well that in this delicate matter they shouldn't do anything without consulting us.

CHAMBERLAIN: They will consult us, I am sure they will. What shall we tell Flandin when he flies over?

BALDWIN: I shall make it clear to him that we are not ready for war.

CHAMBERLAIN: He might argue that removing the Germans from the Rhineland is a mere police operation.

BALDWIN: I shall tell him in no uncertain terms that if there is one chance in a hundred that war might result from his police operation, I have no right to commit Great Britain. The reality is that neither France nor Great Britain is in a position to take effective military action against Germany. Flandin knows that too. If he has forgotten it, I shall remind him.

CHAMBERLAIN: I think the press has been very responsible.

BALDWIN: We can't complain.

CHAMBERLAIN: *The Times* specifically refrains from calling the German move an 'aggression'.

BALDWIN: On the other hand they call it flagrant. That may not help us if we want to wriggle out of the Locarno guarantee.

CHAMBERLAIN: There is no question of wriggling out. You know.

BALDWIN: Yes, I suppose so. The conclusion in the *Times* leader is clear. Just what I would have said myself. 'The old structure of European peace, one-sided and unbalanced, is nearly in ruins. It is the moment not to despair, but to rebuild.' This is exactly what we need to do. The leader in the *Manchester Guardian* was quite reasonable too. It says that for the 'Germans to insist on defending their own territory is not the same heinous moral offence as the attack on Abyssinia'.

CHAMBERLAIN: Quite so.

BALDWIN: And their emphasis is on 'cleaning up the horrible mess of suspicion and fear, which has poisoned these last few years, and to do it somehow with Germany, since it is obvious that it cannot be done without her.'

CHAMBERLAIN: Yes, very reasonable all round. I agree with all of them, even with the leader of the *Manchester Guardian*. Don't you think Stanley that we can be proud of our newspapers? No jingoism. Not a shred of it.

BALDWIN: You know all these press comments are in broad agreement with the advice I received from Arnold Toynbee. He has just returned from a lecture tour in Germany and had a privileged two-hour talk with Hitler. He assures me that the Fuhrer is sincere in his wish for peace in Europe. If this is the well considered opinion of our foremost historian we should not argue with that.

CHAMBERLAIN: No, we shouldn't. We were already thinking along similar lines last year when Eden visited Hitler. Perhaps he should have tried harder to come to some agreement.

BALDWIN: Nothing is lost yet. Sooner or later we shall have to make some conciliatory approaches to Germany. They must now be ready to make some reciprocal concessions. Don't you think that if we accept the remilitarisation of the Rhineland without much ado then they would be willing to sign an 'Air Pact' agreeing to limit their Air Force, similar to the Navy Pact we signed with them recently.

CHAMBERLAIN: Yes, clearly, that should be our aim, and we could surely achieve that provided the French don't make too much noise at the League.

SECRETARY: A Mr Ralph Wigram from the Foreign Office would like to have immediate access to the Prime Minister.

BALDWIN: Show him in.

WIGRAM (ENTERS, OUT OF BREATH): I don't know, Sir, whether you remember me. We met . . .

BALDWIN: Of course, of course. What brings you here?

WIGRAM: I have news from Paris. It will probably be made public in a few hours.

BALDWIN: Radical news?

WIGRAM: Yes, I think so. Firstly, Barthou, Reynaud and Laval have been co-opted to the Cabinet.

BALDWIN: Barthou? An old man in a wheelchair? What is the good of that?

WIGRAM: He is still very influential, Sir.

CHAMBERLAIN: And why Reynaud? Why do they need a financial expert at this time?

WIGRAM: He is more than a financial expert. He has been in favour of rearmament and he is as anti-German as anyone can be.

CHAMBERLAIN: But why Laval? It does not make sense.

BALDWIN: Not as Prime Minister, I presume.

WIGRAM: No, as Minister without portfolio.

BALDWIN: Have they done anything irreparable?

WIGRAM: Not as far as I know. But they might very well decide to do something radical. There is another major shift in the Cabinet I have not mentioned yet. Maurin, the Minister of War, has resigned.

BALDWIN: Was he pushed?

WIGRAM: According to the confidential report I received, Sarraut wanted to force a quite junior officer on him as his Under-Secretary of War.

BALDWIN: Who was it?

WIGRAM: His name is Charles de Gaulle, one of Reynaud's proteges. I doubt you've heard of him. He is 46 years of age—

BALDWIN: Old for a soldier, young for a politician.

WIGRAM: He published a book some two years ago on the need for setting up a professional army in France, and on the merits of tank warfare. When Maurin heard of the proposed appointment he threatened to resign. Whether he meant it or not, I don't know, but his resignation was promptly accepted. We have now an entirely unknown quantity as Minister of War in France.

BALDWIN: Did your source say anything about their intentions to consult us?

WIGRAM: No, nothing at all. With all these changes I would be reluctant to make any predictions.

BALDWIN: Thank you Mr. Wigram. I appreciate the speed with which you have informed us of the latest developments in Paris. (WIGRAM EXITS.) Well, this does not sound to me much of an *entente cordiale*.

CHAMBERLAIN: Not to me either. I would say it is a clear example of a *mesentente discordial*.

BALDWIN: It is. That's what it is. (PAUSE.) We must call a Cabinet meeting.

SCENE 4

SARRAUT: Messieurs. Today is decision day. I think my radio broadcast was well received. There were hardly any dissenting voices. Even the right-wing press was reasonable. *Le Temps* was quite explicit, wasn't it? I presume you have all read the article: (READING WITH EMPHASIS.) 'Once again Germany presented Europe with the fait accompli of unilateral denunciation of a treaty it freely signed.' And then later: 'It is sufficient to read the text of Articles 42 and 43 of the Locarno Treaty to realise the gravity of the situation.' They mixed up Versailles and Locarno but that's beside the point. The important thing is that the country is behind us. That will help us to make a decision. The first question is whether we should rely on the appeal I have already made to the League of Nations and wait for the outcome or have a quick military response. The second question is whether we should go ahead on our own or make military action dependent on British support. Question number 3 is a technical one. Should we order a general or partial mobilisation? The fourth question is a purely military one beyond the competence of most of us. Where should we attack, and with what force?

FLANDIN: We need Britain. It would be so much preferable for the two Western democracies to act in unison. Shouldn't I fly over and consult them? There's no harm in simply exploring their reactions.

SARRAUT: Assume that we ask for military support. They will say that they are not in a position to undertake any military commitments. If we ask for moral support, they will say, 'Yes, certainly, we shall support you with all our might,' which would mean fine speeches at the League of Nations. Do we want that? If we are prepared to wait for a decision by the Council of the League of Nations, then yes, there is much to recommend M. Flandin's visit to London.

BARTHOU (SPEAKS SLOWLY AND WITH DIFFICULTY): We have not got the time.

MANDEL: Yes, time is of the essence.

FLANDIN: If we go ahead with general mobilisation without consulting the British that will only accentuate the anti-French sentiment we have so often come across in England since the end of the war.

MANDEL: Consulting takes time. Consultation is not something you can suddenly interrupt. You can give an ultimatum to an enemy: 'Clear out or we attack.' But not to a friend. Once we have asked for their opinion we shall have to wait for their reply. And that takes time.

BARTHOU (SLOWLY): We have not got the time. Unless we attack in the next few days we lose our momentum.

SARRAUT: It all depends on how the British will interpret the phrase 'flagrant violation of Articles 42 and 43?'

FLANDIN: Surely it **is** a flagrant violation.

SARRAUT: Yes, of course, but will the British think so? Will they try to escape from their obligations? What do you think, General de Gaulle?

DE GAULLE: I am overawed by the title of General. I need to get used to it. It's only been a couple of hours—Excuse me (PAUSE.). I am very reluctant to express an opinion in such august company. I am a soldier, not a politician.

SARRAUT: But if I push you to tell us your sincere opinion.

DE GAULLE: Very well. I don't trust the British. They are insular, they are a maritime power. Britain is linked through her exchanges, her markets, her supply lines to the most diverse and often the most distant countries. And I would not even be sure where they stand between France and Germany, particularly after the ratification of the Franco-Soviet mutual assistance pact. British policy has always been based on the balance of power on the Continent. They might prefer an Anglo-German alliance to an Anglo-French one.

MANDEL: This is Hitler's argument in *Mein Kampf.*

DE GAULLE: I have never read *Main Kampf.*

MANDEL: You should. You will find phrases like 'the inexorable mortal enemy of the German people is and remains France'.

DE GAULLE: I don't need to read *Mein Kampf* to appreciate the German Government's perception of our country.

SARRAUT: Messieurs, could we return to the likely attitude of the British?

DE GAULLE: Britain has always stood up for her own interests. If it suits her she will abandon us for an Anglo-German alliance.

MANDEL: Nonsense. Britain will never align herself with Nazi Germany. Absolute nonsense.

SARRAUT: Thank you, General, for your assessment of the situation. As you say, you are a soldier, not a politician. Your contribution will be of enormous importance when we discuss matters military. Now could we have a few more opinions. Yes, M. Barthou.

BARTHOU: I do believe in collective security. I think I did more than anybody else to make the Franco-Soviet treaty a reality. I think the British position is irrelevant. It matters not what they think or what they plan to do. We must act whether England pledges her support or not.

SARRAUT: Yes M. Reynaud.

REYNAUD: I agree with M. Barthou. We must act.

SARRAUT: M. Laval?

LAVAL: I fear that we shall make a fatal mistake. By taking military action now we shall jeopardize for the immediate future, and may be for ever, any possibility of a Franco-German rapprochement. I share General de Gaulle's feeling that we cannot count on the British. And going alone? It's far too risky.

SARRAUT: Are you in favour of a wait-and-see policy, or to start negotiations immediately with Germany?

LAVAL: The latter. We have been presented with a brutal fait accompli, I agree. It's an insult, I don't deny it. But let us face the facts. Whether we like it or not Germany by the sheer weight of its population, by its industrial potential is or will soon be the most powerful country in Europe. We might chase them out of the Rhineland now, but they will come back. You cannot keep a great nation down for ever. I don't want to argue that Versailles was a mistake, although it probably was. I want to talk about the future. To achieve peace in Europe and in the world an understanding with Germany is absolutely necessary. We could go to the League if we must, but on no account should we upset the Germans. We could use the present impasse as a bargaining chip. If we accept with good grace the fait accompli, we could in exchange have a Franco-German non-aggression pact. Chancellor Hitler may not be a democrat at home, but his foreign policy has been perfectly reasonable. He knows the value of alliances. We should have an agreement with him before he negotiates various treaties with the British, like the recent naval agreement which they concluded behind our backs. Do we need a better example of insincerity? I agree with General de Gaulle. We cannot count on the British. As the Marquis de Ximenez said—

DE GAULLE: Perfidious Albion.

LAVAL: La perfide Albion.

SARRAUT: Does anyone wish to explore the chances of a speedy reconciliation with Germany? I myself am strongly against it. (PAUSE.) Anyone for it? (PAUSE.) I think we should reject that option. So what have we got left? Military intervention.

FLANDIN: We should consult the British.

MANDEL: If we wish to have British support it is best not to consult them. If we consult them they will advise caution. If we go ahead with the military option they will, I have no doubts about it, discharge their treaty obligations.

SARRAUT: With moderate enthusiasm?

MANDEL: Yes, with moderate enthusiasm.

SARRAUT (TO MANDEL): You may very well be right. We'll see. What do you think General? Risk going ahead without the support of perfidious Albion? Do you think our officers are ready for conflict? Our military philosophy, stated frequently by our Chief of Staff and by all the generals of the last war, has been purely defensive.

DE GAULLE: I would call that *sclerose doctrinale*, the views of our insipid, uninspired generals. That's not how our rank and file officers see military strategy. It is just not true that they have been trained to do nothing else but to sit in comfortable bunkers and wait for the enemy to attack. That's not **our** military philosophy. I have attended many a military exercise at the Ecole Superieure de Guerre. I can tell you that out of fifteen exercises only two were defensive. My men will know what to do.

SARRAUT: Could I conclude from what you've said that you are in favour of military action?

DE GAULLE: Yes, yes, of course.

REYNAUD, BARTHOU (SIMULTANEOUSLY): Quite right . . . Yes, Yes.

SARRAUT: Thank you, General. I am glad to hear your views. I have had no doubts that in our hour of need the officer corps will rise to the task. I am glad to have your assurances, General, that they are well prepared. Is there now a consensus in favour of military action?

LAVAL: I cannot condone such action.

SARRAUT: Anybody else against it? Yes, M. Deat. What is the view of the Minister of the Air Force?

DEAT: With the present strength of our fighter planes we could not even defend Paris against German bombers. We should not be irresponsible. We can't run the risk of war when we are so unprepared.

REYNAUD: Nonsense. You are greatly overestimating the German Air Force. Hitler has been in power for three years and one month. Believe me, nobody can create an Air Force in that time. They might have superiority in a few years time but not now, not yet. I am not worried about the Germans bombing Paris.

MANDEL: I think the risk of prolonged conflict is negligible if we act now. It must be clear to everybody that Hitler is bluffing. We may be unprepared but so are the Germans. Who do you think is actually occupying the cities in the Rhineland? Raw recruits who will run at the first opportunity, and superannuated officers with bad eyesight and beer-bellies. We must call Hitler's bluff.

LAVAL: It is irresponsible.

MANDEL: It is irresponsible not to act. If we resist the occupation of the Rhineland by force the German Army will depose Hitler.

LAVAL: They would not dare to raise a hand against him.

MANDEL: They will. But even if every conspiring Army officer was struck down by Spanish influenza, Germany would still be unable to conduct a war beyond a week at most. Nazi Germany, in contrast to that of the Kaiser, has no financial resources. There will be a run on the mark. Their financial system will collapse.

LAVAL: And so would ours. M. Reynaud, you are a financial expert. Tell us, can we sustain a prolonged war?

REYNAUD: Not on our own but we can count on the Anglo-Saxons.

LAVAL: You think we can?

REYNAUD: Yes, I am sure. I know you didn't quite mean it but still I have been appalled by those sardonic references to la perfide Albion. Britain will stand with us and so will the Americans. I know, I was in the United States a couple of years ago. I gave some lectures. I was offered tremendous support everywhere, every single time, when I said that our great democracies must work together to thwart the designs of the dictators. The Americans came to our help in '17, remember? If it comes to a long war they will intervene in good time. And there are the Russians too.

SARRAUT: I think we should leave the Russians out of consideration.

BARTHOU: But surely we can count on the Czechs and the Poles. Has the Foreign Office had some response from them?

FLANDIN: Not yet, I'm afraid, not yet.

BARTHOU: Didn't both Governments offer help if it came to a shooting war?

FLANDIN: Nothing definite.

BARTHOU: If we intervene they will support us militarily. That will be their chance to get rid of the German danger for the foreseeable future. With firm assurances from Eastern Europe would M. Laval be in favour of action?

LAVAL: First of all let me tell you that the Czechs won't fight. The last battle they fought was at the White Mountain in 1618. Secondly—

BARTHOU: Well, they have had a good rest since 1618 but I am sure that now in 1936 they recognise the German danger as much as we do. They have the means to attack, their tanks are among the best in the world, they have the motivation, and they have the will.

LAVAL: May be. But even if the Czechs turn out to have not only the best tanks but also the best soldiers in the world that would not make the slightest difference in the long run. Sooner or later we shall have to face the might of Germany. We shall pay dearly if we make a mistake now. I shall not be part of such a misguided adventure.

SARRAUT: Apart from Messieurs Laval and Deat is anybody else against military action? (PAUSE.) In that case—

LAVAL: I regret, I cannot go along with you. I have to offer my resignation as the recently co-opted minister without portfolio.

SARRAUT: It would be a great loss to the Cabinet. Can I prevail on you to change your mind? We should not be deprived of your advice.

LAVAL: I shall speak tomorrow in the Chamber. (STANDS UP.) Everyone will be able to hear my advice.

DEAT (STANDS UP): I must join M. Laval.

LAVAL AND DEAT EXIT.

SCENE 5

SARRAUT: Well, we are probably better off without them. Let's get down to the details. Full mobilisation or partial mobilisation? Am I right that we are not keen on a general mobilisation? What do you propose, General?

DE GAULLE: Partial mobilisation. We don't need to add to the bulk of the Army. We should call up all those with skills to make us more mobile, we shall need all the explosives experts, we need to call up all those who have already served in the Rhineland when we last occupied it, and we have to bring to the front line all the tanks we have, all of them without exception. Our Char B is vastly superior to any tank the Germans have.

(KNOCK ON THE DOOR, SECRETARY ENTERS)

SECRETARY: Excuse me, Messieurs, there is an urgent 'phone call for M. Flandin. It is M. Krofta the Czechoslovak Foreign Minister on the line.

SARRAUT: Take it here.

FLANDIN: Yes, it's Flandin.

KROFTA (METALLIC SOUND ON THE TELEPHONE): Bonjour. I can now give a definite answer to yesterday's question. You wanted to know what the Czechoslovak Government would do if French troops crossed the German border.

FLANDIN: I am all ears.

KROFTA: I am authorised to tell you that we shall order general mobilisation. We shall be able to attack German positions 72 hours after you move into action.

FLANDIN: I knew we could count on the Czechoslovak Army. I shall tell M. Sarraut immediately.

KROFTA: Tell him that we were greatly impressed by his speech.

FLANDIN: Thank you I shall tell him. He'll be pleased. I shall keep you informed. We shall send instructions about the details to our ambassador in Prague. Au revoir. (HANGS UP.) Messieurs, this is important news. With the support of the Czechoslovak Army, I believe they can muster 35 divisions, the whole exercise seems less of a gamble.

DE GAULLE: I am pleased to hear that we can count on the Czechs but we don't need them. France on her own is perfectly capable of taking on Nazi Germany. I do not regard this operation as a gamble. I agree with M. Mandel that at the present strength of German military preparedness we should not have any difficulties. We can dislodge them within a week at worst. I have got plans, Messieurs, for the offensive. It should be on a narrow front with overwhelming force. We shall move in tank after tank and destroy everything that looks vaguely military. We shall blow up all barracks and all police stations in our way. We shall make it crystal clear that we mean business.

SARRAUT: Have you got a clear idea of where to attack?

DE GAULLE: Yes, I have a good idea but I would like to have some up-to-date information first. I shall order reconnaissance aircraft to fly over the Rhineland. The first one to fly by dawn tomorrow.

SARRAUT: Are you confident that the Germans will not shoot them down?

DE GAULLE: Yes, I am confident. The last thing they want to do is to provoke us. The tables have been turned Messieurs. Now it is their turn to worry. I shall give all the orders in the next few hours and report tomorrow morning.

SCENE 6

BALDWIN: Events seem to have moved quite fast, haven't they?

CHAMBERLAIN: They have.

BALDWIN: The French keep us informed of their moves, but that's all.

CHAMBERLAIN: We are on the edge of the precipice. Partial mobilisation, troop movements, requisition of trains, red alert at all airports.

BALDWIN: General mobilisation in Czechoslovakia or at least preparations for it.

CHAMBERLAIN: I wonder how much time we have before we receive a call to discharge our treaty obligations.

BALDWIN: Soon, I expect, too soon. Your brother should have had more sense than to sign that document.

CHAMBERLAIN: It seemed a good idea at the time.

BALDWIN: There's no escape now. We have to call up some reserves and—

CHAMBERLAIN: Incur the wrath of the pacifists, of the pro-Germans and of all those who dislike our neighbour across the Channel.

BALDWIN: We are lucky that Lansbury, that raving pacifist, is no longer the Leader of the Labour Party. You should talk to Major Attlee.

CHAMBERLAIN: Why me?

BALDWIN: As the next Prime Minister. I shall go to the Palace tonight to offer my resignation.

CHAMBERLAIN: Why in such a hurry? You could wait for developments.

BALDWIN: No thanks. I would have had to resign one of these days, whatever happened in the world. You know that my health is not as robust as it used to be, especially my hearing. If you don't mind I shall propose to the King that he ask you to form the next Government.

CHAMBERLAIN: Wouldn't Winston be a better choice at such a juncture?

BALDWIN: Certainly not! He could be offered the Admiralty if you are so inclined, but I wouldn't do so myself. He always wants to do something spectacular like the relief of Antwerp in '14 or the Dardanelles in the year after. I bet the first thing he would do would be to blockade the ports of Hamburg and Bremen, possibly with disastrous consequences.

CHAMBERLAIN: Perhaps we should leave Winston out of the Cabinet.

BALDWIN: As you like. I wish I knew what to do. Things may turn nasty. You might want to form a Government of National Unity.

SCENE 7

CHAMBERLAIN: Major Attlee, how kind of you to give up your time.

ATTLEE: Thank you for the invitation.

CHAMBERLAIN: As you know, I am trying to form a Government of National Unity. The hostilities have already started. We have dispatched to Metz a token force of two infantry brigades and a squadron of light bombers. They may see action at any moment. Now is the time to bury party differences. If a formal declaration of war becomes necessary, will you vote for it in the House?

ATTLEE: Your decision to honour the Locarno Pact is highly commendable. We can understand why the French are in a hurry. But the Labour movement would never vote for war unless authorised by the Council of the League of Nations.

CHAMBERLAIN: I agree. Approval by the League is of the utmost importance. The chances are high that the Assembly will, with an overwhelming majority, declare Germany to be in breach of the Locarno Treaty.

ATTLEE: I am aware of that, but please note finding Germany in breach of a treaty is not the same as declaring war on Germany. We should not leave any stone unturned in our search for peace. It was a mistake to send troops—

CHAMBERLAIN: Just a symbolic gesture.

ATTLEE: However restricted the number, we should not have moved any of our forces into the war zone without the explicit approval of the Council of the League of Nations.

CHAMBERLAIN: I fully share your anxiety. I have always been in favour of negotiations with Germany. I am sure I could find a peaceful solution if I had a chance to sit down with Herr Hitler. But after the French move our only option is to support them.

ATTLEE: Our cause is just. But we have to go through the proper channels. It is not for us to decide whether Germany did or did not violate a particular treaty or if she did, what kind of action should be taken by members of the League.

CHAMBERLAIN: But France has decided to act. Sarraut maintains that aggression should be immediately answered by force. I don't agree with him, but what could we do? Should we have ignored their call for help? Should we have declined to honour our treaty obligations?

ATTLEE: It is up to the Government to decide. The Labour movement cannot compromise its principles. We are a party of peace.

END OF ACT TWO

ACT 3

THE AFTERMATH

ACT 3, SCENE 1

DE GAULLE (ON THE TELEPHONE): General de Gaulle reporting. Is that M. Sarraut?

SARRAUT: It is.

DE GAULLE: You may be interested in a brief progress report.

SARRAUT: It's high time.

DE GAULLE: Sorry, I was out of range of radio communications most of the time and in any case this is not something for the radio. Now I have a safe telephone line to Metz. I am at the outskirts of Kaiserlautern, 40 km over the French border.

SARRAUT: Good. Good. May I now hear your report.

DE GAULLE: It has been a walkover so far. It has been ten hours.

SARRAUT: Ten critical hours.

DE GAULLE: Not really. We started at dawn at four hundred hours. In fact, it was quite difficult to find any enemy. The German occupying forces had five days to build some fortifications. I would have done that in their place but they did nothing. When we appeared on the scene the German troops have just melted away.

SARRAUT: No resistance at all?

DE GAULLE: No resistance worth mentioning, not so far anyway.

SARRAUT: Perhaps you could still give me an account of some incidents however insignificant they might have been.

DE GAULLE: Yes, of course. A few skirmishes and one minor encounter, an ambush I might say. It happened at Waderborn at a small bridge across the Prim. I was there earlier in the morning. By the time I arrived a young Lieutenant and about a dozen soldiers lay dead on the ground.

SARRAUT: Germans ?

DE GAULLE: Yes, Germans. One fell in the brook. Not that it helped him much. When we pulled him out he was dead too.

SARRAUT: What happened?

DE GAULLE: The young Lieutenant apparently wanted to make a stand at the bridge. Poor sod, but for Hitler he would be still alive. They fired an anti-aircraft gun at one of our Char Bs. They aimed quite well, scored two hits but as you would expect the shells just bounced off. There are two small dents, that's all. When the turret responded all those handling the gun were dead. I could give you an even more graphic description if you wanted one.

SARRAUT: No, thank you, that would not be necessary. What are our casualties?

DE GAULLE: Light, very light indeed. Six dead, ten or eleven wounded, five killed by enemy fire, the sixth one run over by a Renault FT-17, our own light tank. Did good service in the Great War, by now they are a bit unreliable. The brake was faulty and the young man was a little slow. Problem of maintenance, you know. These things happen. I am writing in person to the next of kin.

SARRAUT: As things went so easily I hope you countermanded your order of burning all police stations on the way.

DE GAULLE: As a matter of fact, I did. There was no point striking terror in their hearts when they were running away as fast as they could.

SARRAUT: So how many stations did you burn down?

DE GAULLE: Only two, in two villages. None in Saarbrucken. The people were quite friendly

SARRAUT: Good. Very good. What next?

DE GAULLE: My plan is to stop this evening at about 1800 hours some 20 km from the Rhine. If resistance continues to be so weak I would not mind having a look at the Rhine myself later today.

SARRAUT: Don't expose yourself too much to enemy fire. France needs you.

DE GAULLE: I'll be careful, don't worry. I know perfectly well what I am doing. I am not expecting any surprises. You can have a quiet night.

SARRAUT: D'you think you could ring me at eight o'clock tonight?

DE GAULLE: Yes, certainly.

ACT 3, SCENE 2

MANDEL ALONE IN HIS ROOM

(TELEPHONE RINGS.)

MANDEL: Yes.

SARRAUT (VOICE HEARD ON THE TELEPHONE.): It's me.

MANDEL: Have you had a second report from the General?

SARRAUT: I have.

MANDEL: And?

SARRAUT: Everything is quiet. We are in control. Two brigades reached the Rhine.

MANDEL: Fantastic. Anything else.

SARRAUT: Yes, I have some more good news for you.

MANDEL: Tell me.

SARRAUT: Guess.

MANDEL: I can't.

SARRAUT: Hitler is under house arrest.

MANDEL: No.

SARRAUT: Yes. It has been announced by the Reichsrundfunk ten minutes ago.

MANDEL: Fantastic. What happened?

SARRAUT: Guess.

MANDEL: The Army?

SARRAUT: Yes, an Army coup.

MANDEL: Great. Long live the Royal Prussian Army.

SARRAUT: They haven't changed an iota since the days of Frederick the Great, have they? The same proud people.

MANDEL: No, they haven't changed. Not at all. Shall we drink a toast to German militarism?

SARRAUT: We shall. They are sensible fellows.

MANDEL: Who is behind the coup? Anyone we know?

SARRAUT: Blomberg, their Minister of War.

MANDEL: Who they call a Siegfried with a monocle?

SARRAUT: Yes.

MANDEL: The man who made the officer corps swear a personal oath of loyalty to Adolf Hitler?

SARRAUT: The very same man. Apparently his love for his master was not unconditional. And Fritsch.

MANDEL: The Commander in Chief of the Army?

SARRAUT: Yes. Well, I must say, events have completely justified our response.

MANDEL: I predicted that, didn't I?

SARRAUT: Yes, you did.

MANDEL: It wasn't a particularly difficult prediction. Any student of psychology would have come to the same conclusion. Prussian officers don't like taking orders from an ex-corporal (HIS VOICE RISES AS HE SPEAKS.), an adventurer, a nobody, a madman, a criminal—

SARRAUT: And particularly not when the ex-corporal wants to teach them how to wage war.

MANDEL: I knew the Army would not be willing participant in such gamble. Poor old Hitler. Like the English say: he tried to teach his grandmother how to suck eggs. I don't think many tears will be shed for little Adolf Hitler and fat Hermann Goering. Didn't they look ridiculous as heirs to the German Empire?

SARRAUT: They did indeed.

MANDEL: I presume the new German government has asked for a ceasefire.

SARRAUT: Yes, an immediate ceasefire. At the same time Blomberg ordered all military units to withdraw behind the Rhine.

MANDEL: Shouldn't we demand the withdrawal of German troops to the line 50 km to the East of the Rhine, as stipulated by the Versailles Treaty?

SARRAUT: I don't think it would be politic to do that just now. Let's not make any demands on the German military until the situation stabilises.

MANDEL: What d'you intend to do?

SARRAUT. I shall make an announcement on the radio tonight, tell the Germans that our quarrel was with the Nazis and not with the German people, and that we shall withdraw our troops at our earliest opportunity.

MANDEL: Within a week?

SARRAUT: Why not?.

ACT 3, SCENE 3

NARRATOR: The bloody counter-coup started the day after at ten o'clock at night. Army patrols in every major city were ambushed by heavily armed members of the SS in civilian clothes. In Berlin the building of the Ministry of War was stormed by teenagers of the Hitler Jugend. Adolf Hitler was found unhurt in a darkened room in the East Wing. The first one to greet him was Baldur von Schirach. 'Heil Hitler,' he cried, 'My young men have done their duty to the Fatherland.'

NARRATOR 2: Adolf Hitler addressed the German nation the following morning.

HITLER: If I speak to you today it is first in order that you should hear my voice and that you should know that I myself am unhurt and well. Second in order that you should know more about a crime unparalleled in German history. A very small clique of ambitious, irresponsible, mad and criminally stupid officers had the audacity to raise a hand against me, threaten my life and usurp power for over 24 hours. Thanks to the heroism of the SS and of the Hitler Youth, led by our fearless comrade-in-arms, Baldur von Schirach, we have turned the table on the traitors and on their accomplices. I want to tell you that the gang of filthy criminals is now under guard and will answer for their betrayal of Germany at the People's Court later today. We shall get quits with them in the way that National Socialists are accustomed. I am convinced that every decent officer, every gallant soldier, will comprehend this at this hour. What fate would have been in store for Germany had this putsch succeeded is too horrible to think of. My life is only one of care and labour for my people. I shall go on bearing these cares and to continue with my labour to act according to the dictates of my conscience. It has been granted to me that I should escape a fate which would have been terrible, not for me, but for the German people. We can all see in this the pointing figure of Providence that I must and will carry on with my work.

ACT 3, SCENE 4

JOURNALIST: Germany has had so many upheavals in the recent past. The British public is greatly interested in your views, Dr. Goebbels. What do you think the main reasons are for the repeated attacks on German sovereignty?

GOEBBELS: We have been victims of unprovoked attacks all through our history and particularly from our neighbour in the West. You know who I am thinking about. As the Fuhrer has repeatedly pointed out the aim of French policy, whoever the rulers were, whether Bourbons or Jacobins, Bonapartists or bourgeois democrats, clerical republicans or Social Democrats has always been to seize possession of the Rhine border and to secure this watercourse for France by means of a dismembered and shattered Germany. The genius of Count Bismarck made this country strong and united. The war of 1870-71 and that of 1914-18 were clearly due to French intransigence and their desire to encircle Germany. The present Franco-Soviet Pact is an exact copy of their pact with Tsarist Russia. The British public knows very well the iniquities of the Versailles Treaty. You see what happens when we try to loosen, just a little, the ropes with which Germany has been bound ever since Versailles. We must loosen those ropes just to avoid suffocation, just to be able to breath more freely. The response is aggression, sheer, unmitigated aggression. We have sent into the Rhineland a small symbolic force of lightly armed men and the French have responded by deploying seven divisions supported by hundreds of tanks.

With traitors in our midst, in the high command of the Army which has the duty to protect the Fatherland, we were powerless to resist the French assault.

JOURNALIST: Do you think that the French had a hand in inciting the Army leaders to rebel.

GOEBBELS: Undoubtedly. We know now that both Blomberg and Fritsch, the leaders of the Army putsch, were French agents. They confessed everything before they were executed. True they could hold on to power for a little over 24 hours but then the wrath of the German people swept them away.

JOURNALIST: With French troops stationing on the Rhine how do you see the future?

GOEBBELS: Peace is Germany's solemn desire. We have no territorial claims against any other nation in Europe or anywhere in the world. All we want is to live in peace and harmony under the leadership of the Fuhrer.

JOURNALIST: What is the message I can convey from you to the British public?

GOEBBELS: I know of your anti-war demonstrations. I am one with the British people in desiring peace. Put pressure on your government to withdraw British troops from the Rhineland. Why should Britain so slavishly follow French militarism? Your opposition parties, the Liberals and the Labour Party are solidly against the war, against adventurism, against French incursions into German territory. I gather from your newspapers that in any new election the clique of warmongers around Chamberlain will not be re-elected. Press for new elections if you want to preserve peace in Europe. That is my message to the British people.

ACT 3, SCENE 5

NARRATOR1: A month has passed since the coup and the counter-coup. In spite of expectations the population of the Rhineland was not unfriendly towards the occupying French troops. On the fifth Sunday a small crowd gathered around the Market Square in the historic city of Kaiserlautern. It consisted mainly of pensioners and children happy to listen to the regular Sunday morning performance of the military band of the 2nd Grenadiers. The band's favourites were military songs going back to the Revolution headed, naturally, by the Marseillaise but by the fifth Sunday, in order to please their German hosts, they could produce quite passable versions of some German military songs from the Great War like (SINGING.) 'Ich hatt' einen Kameraden, einen bessern finds du nicht'. On that particular Sunday they wanted to go even further. They planned something spectacular, a rendition of the Ride of the Valkyrie, which no military band had ever attempted before. The second half of the performance started with a little solo by the drummer, a corporal well under twenty. Three little girls were so eager to satisfy their curiosity concerning the origin of those majestic sounds that they sneaked into the cordoned off area and stopped in sheer admiration in front of the drummer. When the French horn joined in, suddenly a bevy of young, angel-faced boys appeared in white shirts and brown ties, each one carrying a school satchel. They approached Market Square from the direction of the local Lutheran Church. They sang, rather out of tune, a hymn to the greater glory of God. The drummer stopped drumming, the French horn fell into silence. As if in sympathy the boys stopped singing as well. But then, with practised moves, they opened their satchels, took out the hand grenades, pulled the safety pins and hurled them over the crowd into the middle of the band. Practised they may have been in the art of throwing hand grenades but the technical back-up did not reach the same perfection. Only one of the hand grenades went off killing instantly the drummer and the three little girls. The leader of the band was quick to respond. He unbuttoned his revolver-case, drew the safety catch and fired six shots at the fleeing children. One fell, the rest rapidly disappeared around the corner. Next day, the front page of the Volkischer Beobachter, the official journal of the National Socialist German Workers Party carried the headline. 'Kaiserlautern Massacre. Four German Children Killed by French troops.'

ACT 3, SCENE 6

JOURNALIST: M. le President du Conseil des Ministres, the readers of my newspaper in Britain are greatly concerned with the steadily deteriorating situation on the West Bank of the Rhine. Allied troops have been occupying the territory for over four months. Can you see any benefits coming from that?

SARRAUT: Yes, **our** troops are there and not those of the Wehrmacht.

JOURNALIST: Your casualties have recently reached one hundred dead. Was it worth the lives of one hundred French soldiers just to prevent the Germans from moving into their own back garden?

SARRAUT: We had to act.

JOURNALIST: Are you satisfied with the present state of affairs?

SARRAUT: No.

JOURNALIST: Do you think the time has come to withdraw French troops from German soil?

SARRAUT: No.

JOURNALIST: According to Dr. Goebbels your troops have killed 263 boys between the ages of 14 and 18 so far.

SARRAUT: Our figures are actually 24. Those were boys killed while throwing hand grenades or shooting at our soldiers. It is regrettable that such young boys have taken up arms but we always shoot back whenever we are shot at.

JOURNALIST: But do you admit that your military intelligence arrested hundreds of young boys?

SARRAUT: A few boys found in possession of weapons have indeed been arrested. They might number a few dozen but certainly no more. Dr. Goebbels' figures are hardly ever accurate.

JOPURNALIST: D'you agree that this situation is entirely our own making? The occupation of the West Bank of the Rhineland by the allied troops has radicalised the Nazi movement. Now we reap the consequences of our actions. We have transformed Boy Scouts into killers.

SARRAUT: I don't think that the Hitler Youth could have been compared with Boy Scouts at the best of times. They have been brainwashed from an early age.

JOURNALIST: What do you mean brainwashed?

SARRAUT: Brainwashed are the people who are told the same thing again and again until they become fanatical believers. In the present case the belief is in the superiority of the Teutonic race. You and your readers may have heard of the idea of the Herrenvolk.

JOURNALIST: If those young men are so fanatical how do you think you can stop these deadly attacks?

SARRAUT: Plans of this kind are worked out by the allied military council headed by General de Gaulle. You can ask him but it is very unlikely that you will get an answer. We are not in the habit of broadcasting our military plans.

JOURNALIST: Your conduct of the war has been criticised in France by parties both on the Left and on the Right. Your majority in the Chamber of Deputies is meagre to say the least. Do you intend to resign?

SARRAUT: No.

JOURNALIST: So what will you do?

SARRAUT: Continue the same policy.

JOURNALIST: Do you realise it is a bad policy?

SARRAUT: Yes.

JOURNALIST: Then why do you soldier on?

SARRAUT: I continue the same policy because it is the best policy available, the best one under the circumstances. The alternatives are worse. I am determined to stick to the present policy and that's the unanimous view of the Cabinet as well. Now if you will excuse me, I have a meeting to attend.

It was a pleasure to talk to you. You can tell your readers that I appreciate the support of the British Government.

ACT 3, SCENE 7

SARRAUT: I don't think we can do it.

MANDEL: It's difficult.

DE GAULLE: Are you afraid of the international implications?

SARRAUT: Well, yes, that as well.

DE GAULLE: Have you any other idea?

SARRAUT: Well, no. I mean—

MANDEL: We are in an absolutely awful situation.

DE GAULLE: We know that. The question is what to do.

MANDEL: I don't know. I don't know.

DE GAULLE: I don't see any other way forward. We cannot just sit here and do nothing. As our casualty figures mount, it reached two hundred yesterday, the press comments are becoming more and more critical. And the situation isn't much better in the Chamber. Just this week Laval had quite a sympathetic hearing when he demanded the immediate withdrawal of all our troops. Do we want that?

MANDEL: We are all in favour of that provided the Germans undertake that no military personnel and no ammunition will ever cross the Rhine, and let us have observers at every bridge.

SARRAUT: Or observers by the League of Nations.

DE GAULLE: Yes, yes, but Hitler is not willing to negotiate. Let's leave the League of Nations out of it. There is nothing they can do unless everybody agrees. And if everybody agrees there is no need for the League. I strongly feel that the present stalemate simply cannot continue. After six months in the West Bank the French public expects us to be in control. We have to act without delay and in a manner that will make the Germans think again. We taught them a lesson in '18; they are in urgent need of another lesson.

SARRAUT: I agree but—

DE GAULLE: They send over children to throw grenades at us. We cannot prevent that. We cannot search every boy between the ages of 14 and 18 for hidden weapons. The question is simply this; how can we dissuade the Germans from waging this bloody campaign against us? It's not much good to say 'Please keep your eager gangs of Hitler Youth on your side of the Rhine', is it? They won't stop those raids if we ask them nicely, will they? We have to hit them where it hurts. We shall choose a busy industrial district, say in Essen, and direct at it a few dozen salvoes from our heavy guns every single day until they stop the atrocities against our troops.

MANDEL: Can't you think of any other deterrent?

DE GAULLE: I can. We could kill every single German of the male sex between the ages of 14 and 18. A kind of Old Testament justice. That would constitute a perfect deterrent. D'you want that?

SARRAUT: We don't have time for silly arguments. Could we return to the bombardment? What if they respond in kind?

DE GAULLE: How can they? There is no French city within the range of German guns.

MANDEL: The bombardment of a major industrial district could precipitate a real war.

DE GAULLE: If only it **would** precipitate a real war. Unfortunately that is wishful thinking. The Germans will not start it. The Wehrmacht has still not recovered from the purges that followed the failed putsch. All the experienced commanders have been replaced by young SS men who are good at street battles against defenceless people but not so good when facing trained men. And the international situation is even bleaker for them. With 20 Czech divisions ready for action in the border regions of the Erzgebirge, and with the Polish Army poised to descend upon Posen—

MANDEL: That's an unexpected development, isn't it?

DE GAULLE: Quite unexpected. The Poles have suddenly discovered that those old cities around Posen which they call Poznan were taken by the Prussians a century and a half ago and they are determined to restore them to the Motherland.

MANDEL: Amazing. The Poles have now their eyes on territorial gains. Amazing, how historical perspectives change.

DE GAULLE: They do. Would the Germans dare to declare war under the circumstances? They wouldn't. They will either suffer in silence or they will stop the raids.

MANDEL: The effect may be just the opposite. They might step up the raids.

DE GAULLE: If they step up the raids we shall step up the bombardment.

SARRAUT: I don't like it.

DE GAULLE: Have you got anything better to propose?

MANDEL: I have a suggestion.

SARRAUT: What?

MANDEL: Withdraw.

SARRAUT AND DE GAULLE (SIMULTANEOUSLY): Withdraw?

MANDEL: Can we win? That is the question. Do we still believe that we can win? Yes, I know the military balance is in our favour but how long can we sustain the occupation of a chunk of foreign territory? I am slowly coming to the conclusion that we made a mistake, that in our time and age a democracy cannot win against fanatics. We haven't got a chance, We are all doomed.

DE GAULLE: Nonsense. What we need in our time and age is courage and determination. Once you decided on a course of action, stick to it

MANDEL: Assume that we flatten Essen. What shall we achieve with it? Nothing. They will ignore the bombardment and continue their guerrilla attacks. Our casualties will mount and so will the demands to bring our boys back. We cannot control the press. Public opinion will turn against us. Some of our Deputies in the Chamber will vote with the opposition. We lose a vote of confidence. The next government withdraws our troops and comes to an understanding with the Nazis. That's the scenario I dread.

DE GAULLE: That's the scenario of a defeatist. You underestimate the determination of the French people. They will under no circumstances collaborate with a bunch of aggressors.

MANDEL: I hope so. I hope so.

DE GAULLE: The question is simple M. Mandel. The stalemate cannot continue. I refuse to entertain any notion of withdrawal. We shall win.

SARRAUT: Why these sudden doubts M. Mandel? You were the staunchest supporter of intervention in the Cabinet. Why these sudden doubts?

MANDEL: I don't know. I don't know. I am just thinking aloud. I am no longer sure of anything.

SARRAUT: And if we withdraw now, would that be any better? We shall be accused of empty adventurism and lose a vote of confidence anyway.

MANDEL: Maybe. Maybe.

DE GAULLE: There is no need to worry M. Mandel. We shall win. I can assure you.

MANDEL: I don't see how. We cannot control the press. The mood has turned against us. And I can understand that. With over two hundred casualties—

DE GAULLE: We must stay in the Rhineland and put up with the casualties. And we have to find a new initiative. You say it might fail. I am confident that it will not but let us assume that after the bombardment we shall be in an even worse situation with even more casualties. So what! As wars go a few hundred casualties is nothing. I should much rather stay put and have hundreds of casualties now than fight later and have millions.

SARRAUT: It is a major decision. We need to take the matter to the full Cabinet.

DE GAULLE: Nonsense. We don't have time for constitutional niceties.

MANDEL: That would spell the end of the Third Republic.

DE GAULLE: The demise of the Third Republic would not particularly worry me. There will be a Fourth Republic afterwards, and a Fifth. What we want to avoid is the fall of France.

SARRAUT: I don't understand this. You both have an apocalyptic vision of the future.

DE GAULLE: It is just the same vision all of us in the Cabinet had six months ago. If we withdraw now and let them fortify the West Bank we shall let the Germans overrun Europe. Do you want that? Our only chance is to use the bombardment as a deterrent. Would you, please, say yes or no.

MANDEL: I suppose, I must . . .

DE GAULLE: Please, say yes or no.

MANDEL (RELUCTANTLY): Very well.

DE GAULLE: This means yes or no?

MANDEL: Yes.

SARRAUT: Good.

DE GAULLE: I shall take full responsibility for the action. I shall say that it was my initiative, that I did it entirely at my own responsibility. The Cabinet can get rid of me if they wish to.

MANDEL: At least you know what you want to do.

SARRAUT: Fine, go ahead.

ACT 3, SCENE 8

CHAMBERLAIN: It is so kind of you, Stanley, to come. I would have loved to go to your glorious castle alas all my time is taken up nowadays trying to parry the blows coming from various directions.

BALDWIN: I must admit, I don't envy you.

CHAMBERLAIN: I am not in an enviable position.

BALDWIN: I know you have lots of problems now but history will absolve you. You always did the right thing, you always had the interests of the Empire foremost in your mind.

CHAMBERLAIN: You know that, but will posterity know?

BALDWIN: Surely, you will go down in history as one of the great British Prime Ministers.

CHAMBERLAIN: Kind of you to say so. I presume you have followed events closely.

BALDWIN: Most of my time nowadays is devoted to gardening but I still manage to squeeze in the odd bit of newspaper reading.

CHAMBERLAIN: What did you think of de Gaulle's bombing strategy?

BALDWIN: I did not think it would succeed.

CHAMBERLAIN: Did you think that it would be such dismal failure, that after two months of heavy bombardment we should have nothing to show for it?

BALDWIN: Not quite.

CHAMBERLAIN: Flattening Essen and Dusseldorf did not much help our cause, did it?

BALDWIN: No. The Germans simply ignored it and carried on with their guerrilla campaign.

CHAMBERLAIN: And it gained them a lot of sympathy worldwide. The Pope and Cardinal Pacelli made a passionate appeal for showing mercy to young Germans. And Roosevelt, President of the United States, no friend of the Nazis, told the French Ambassador to stop the bombing. No wonder the Italians have changed course. They are now openly and shamelessly supporting the Nazis. Do you know what they now call themselves, the Italians and the Germans? Axis powers.

BALDWIN: Club of Notorious Dictators would be a more appropriate label.

CHAMBERLAIN: I don't mind the Italians, two dictators were going to find each other sooner or later, but I am worried about the situation at home. The funeral of the Essen Three—

BALDWIN: Yes, that was depressing.

CHAMBERLAIN: Three members of that ridiculous ultra-pacifist group who wanted to play the game of human shield, and were mowed down by French shrapnel. Idiots. The sort of people who would not hesitate to kill anybody for the sake of universal peace.

BADLWIN: Kill or be killed. I don't find either alternative appealing.

CHAMBERLAIN: And that anti-war rally after the funeral. Every minute of it was recorded and reported by the press as if it were the most important event in recent history. There was a lot of gratuitous violence. The press loved it. Four arrests. Seven police officers wounded. And to cap it all came the news of two British soldiers killed in an ambush. The first fatal casualties we suffered since we sent our troops there—

BALDWIN: The timing looks too good. It seems likely that Dr. Goebbels ordered the ambush to take place just before the funeral. I think we have underestimated him. That man is capable of anything.

CHAMBERLAIN: You think so.

BALDWIN: Yes, I do. One of the conclusions I came to while digging the garden. Still, we need to be grateful that we have only two dead to the French two hundred.

CHAMBERLAIN: Over two hundred and thirty.

BALDWIN: Hm, that many?

CHAMBERLAIN: You know that Sarraut is going to resign. Who do you think will replace him?

BALDWIN: De Gaulle, surely. It has been on the cards for some time.

CHAMBERLAIN: It is amazing, isn't it? It can only happen in France that a man plucked from obscurity eight months ago can now aim at the highest office in the land.

CHAMBERLAIN: You know I met him last month.

BALDWIN: The papers were full of it.

CHAMBERLAIN: He is apparently the only man who knows what he wants to do. And he would never admit that any of his ideas were ever at fault. I told him, I did not mince my words, I told him that he was responsible for the present situation, that it was his idea to bombard German cities. And I asked him a straight question: 'Can you see now that the bombardment was a big mistake?'

BALDWIN: And what did he reply?

CHAMBERLAIN: You wouldn't believe it. He said that bombardment was the right policy because, as a consequence, it has now become much easier to turn that lukewarm war into a proper war.

BALDWIN: He wants a full-scale war. Ridiculous, quite ridiculous.

CHAMBERLAIN: He envisaged a four-power occupation of Germany by French, British, Polish and Czechoslovak troops.

BALDWIN: That was not in the papers.

CHAMBERLAIN: Fortunately not. There was no leak this time. Imagine what the papers would have made of it.

BALDWIN: I can imagine the headlines. Good thing we were spared of them. Did de Gaulle think that a quick military victory was feasible?

CHAMBERLAIN: He thought German resistance would collapse within two weeks. His main concern was with what happens after victory.

BALDWIN: Quite rightly so.

CHAMBERLAIN: The Poles were to occupy all German territory East of the Odera—Neisse line.

BALDWIN: What's that?

CHAMBERLAIN: Rivers, I think. Or mountains. I have to look them up on the map.

BALDWIN: And the Czechs would do likewise?

CHAMBERLAIN: Yes, somewhere in the East.

BALDWIN: What did he offer us?

CHAMBERLAIN: The North of Germany. He even drew a line somewhere above the Ruhr. Anything above is ours, anything below is theirs.

BALDWIN: Very generous of him. Would we also be granted the privilege of occupying Berlin?

CHAMBERLAIN: No. He was quite specific about Berlin. He wanted to divide the city into four zones, one for each occupying power. He reserved West Berlin and the historical quarter with all the Ministries, etc. to the French. The rest was to be divided between the Poles, the Czechs and ourselves.

BALDWIN: He relegated us to a second-rank power. What damned cheek! Did you tell him what you thought of his ideas?

CHAMBERLAIN: Very politely. I have never been more polite in my life but I made it clear that he should not entertain any hope for British participation in his schemes.

BALDWIN: I don't understand how the mind of this de Gaulle chap works. How did he imagine to keep the whole of Germany occupied when we can't even control the Rhineland? How did he think he could contain the guerrilla campaign?

CHAMBERLAIN: He is not interested in such irrelevant details. I told you. He was full of self-confidence. Never a word of doubt

BALDWIN: Good dictator material.

CHAMBERLAIN: A second Napoleon?

BALDWIN: No, that was the Duke of Reichstadt. De Gaulle will be crowned as Napoleon the Fourth, Emperor of the French or, alternatively, Charles XI, Coeur de Lion, King of France.

CHAMBERLAIN: Not an impossible scenario. Anything can happen in France. You know what galls me above all is that this long-nosed swashbuckler, who, mind you, was with the first troops reaching the Rhine on the first day of operation, this man of daring and pluck, this tactician and strategist, this author of harebrained schemes strongly believes that he incarnates France.

BALDWIN: Yes, (DECLAIMING.) *pour la patrie, pour la gloire*. Yes, he incarnates France all right but he is wrong in thinking that that's something he should be proud of.

CHAMBERLAIN: How do you estimate his chances of forming the next government?

BALDWIN: He might carry it off simply through his personal appeal.

CHAMBERLAIN: The Bonapartist streak?

BALDWIN: That should help in a country like France. However the odds are stacked against him. He will be defeated by an alliance between the left and the right.

CHAMBERLAIN: And that brings me to why I wanted to talk to you in the first place. You will not be surprised to hear that I am at the end of my tether. I want your advice.

BALDWIN: I am at your disposal.

CHAMBERLAIN: Do you think I should resign?

BALDWIN: There is nobody who could take your place.

CHAMBERLAIN: Winston? He would wage this phoney war more energetically.

BALDWIN: There is nothing he could do now. I think we should return to our policy of placating the Germans—exactly what we would have done had not the French forced us to uphold Locarno. If de Gaulle's government is approved in the Chamber you might have to carry on for a while. You can't possibly withdraw our troops. Honour forbids that we should abandon the French in their hour of need.

CHAMBERLAIN: So what is your advice?

BALDWIN: If de Gaulle is confirmed, carry on as best as you can.

CHAMBERLAIN: You mean just grin and bear it. Stanley, I can tell you, I am tired of that incessant, inexorable, utterly dishonest campaign against me, the attacks on my integrity, the cartoons depicting me as a warmonger—

BALDWIN: The likeness was quite good in that cartoon in the *Manchester Guardian* the other day which showed you daintily holding a bloody knife between your teeth.

CHAMBERLAIN: I was not amused.

BALDWIN: If de Gaulle loses the vote of confidence it is quite clear what your best move is.

CHAMBERLAIN: Call an election.?

BALDWIN: Yes, call an election.

CHAMBERLAIN: We are going to lose it.

BALDWIN: Yes, you will have a holiday on the opposition benches.

CHAMBERLAIN: I had thought of that. Is that your honest advice?

BALDWIN: It is. Let Labour and the Liberals form a coalition. They pretend to know what the government should do. Let them do it. They might turn out to be better at appeasement than we were.

ACT 3, SCENE 9

NARRATOR 2 (FEMALE VOICE): De Gaulle's attempt to form the next government at the end of the year of 1936 was heavily defeated in the Chamber of Deputies. The subsequent elections brought to power the Popular Front. New elections held in Britain were also won decisively by the anti-war parties. French and British troops were withdrawn from the West Bank within a month of the elections, followed immediately by the triumphant entry of the newly reconstructed Wehrmacht. The building of the Siegfried line started three days later. In Britain a Lib-Lab coalition was formed with Major Attlee as the Prime Minister. The policy of his government, he declared, was universal peace. The German arms industry suffered major setbacks during the 8 months of occupation mainly due to their inability to secure foreign exchange. However the unity of will among the German people once more led to rapid recovery. Four months after the withdrawal of the allied troops arms production was back at its pre-invasion level. The first combat-ready samples of the more advanced Panzer II rolled off the production line in February 1938.

NARRATOR 1 (MALE VOICE): On the 13ᵗʰ March 1939 German troops moved into Austria where they were enthusiastically received. Osterreich under the name of Ostmark became an integral part of the Third Reich. In September 1939 a four-power conference of Germany, Italy, France and Britain was held in the city of Munich in Bavaria. The conference made great strides towards avoiding war. An agreement was reached between Germany on the one hand and France and Britain on the other hand which allowed Germany to liberate the Sudeten-German population of Czechoslovakia. The document was signed by Prime Ministers Attlee and Daladier. Major Attlee made a triumphant return to England. 'Our negotiations have preserved peace in our time' he declared to the crowd gathered to welcome him at the airport. He did even flaunt the document with Hitler's signature. In March 1940 German troops moved into the rump Czechoslovakia.

Moravia and Bohemia became Reich Protectorates, Slovakia declared independence. The government of Major Attlee underwent a Pauline conversion quite soon after the fall of Czechoslovakia. Britain and France gave guarantees to Poland against a German attack. The Molotov-Ribbentrop agreement was concluded in the latter half of August 1940. Poland was invaded on the 1st September by Germany followed by a Soviet attack two weeks later. France and Britain declared war on Germany. In the spring and summer of 1941 German troops occupied Denmark and Norway and later overran Holland, Belgium and France. Winston Churchill became Prime Minister on the 10th May, 1941. He formed a government of national unity which Attlee was happy to join. General de Gaulle fled to Britain at the end of July. Germany invaded the Soviet Union in the summer of 1942. The United States entered the war at the end of the same year. After many a success of German arms the reverses at El Alamein and Stalingrad signalled the beginning of the end of the Third Reich. The German Army was defeated battle after battle leading to the unconditional surrender of Germany in May 1946. Adolf Hitler committed suicide on the 30th April, 1946. The casualties in the war have been estimated at 50 million dead.

THE END